HOW TO DRAW
Magical, Monstrous & Mythological
CREATURES

Walter Foster

Associate Publisher: Elizabeth T. Gilbert
Managing Editor: Rebecca J. Razo
Art Director: Shelley Baugh
Associate Editor: Emily Green
Production Artists: Debbie Aiken, Rae Siebels
Production Manager: Nicole Szawlowski
International Purchasing Coordinator: Lawrence Marquez

www.walterfoster.com
Walter Foster Publishing, Inc.
3 Wrigley, Suite A
Irvine, CA 92618

1 3 5 7 9 10 8 6 4 2

Table of Contents

CHAPTER 1

Introduction

Magical, monstrous, and mythological creatures are everywhere! Werewolves, vampires, zombies, gargoyles, and mermaids can be found in books, movies, TV shows, and video games. Elves, dragons, and warriors have stepped out of ancient legends and onto everything from T-shirts to backpacks. Most people think these creatures are make-believe. But now you can prove them wrong. All it takes is some creativity, imagination, and a little bit of instruction—thanks to this cool book.

If you've ever wanted to learn to draw those creatures that hide in the shadows, make things go bump in the night, and perform amazing feats like those in legendary tales, now is your chance. From a cell-phone toting vampire, shirt-ripping werewolf, and scythe-wielding Grim Reaper to a creepy bogeyman, slimy swamp creature, and the notorious lightning-bolt thrower, Zeus, the characters featured in these pages will keep your imagination running wild long after you've turned out the lights—and they're just scary enough to keep your little brother or sister from snooping through your room.

Just flip through the pages to discover the secrets of drawing all of your favorite bad guys, step by step. Before you know it, you'll be able to create your own enchanted kingdoms, dark dungeons, and mystical lands.

Here's a chance to put a little magic in your life. So what do you say we get this party started?

Drawing Tools & Materials

• **Sketchpad and Drawing Paper** – Sketchpads come in many sizes and are best for working out your ideas. For finished artwork, use drawing paper.

• **Pencils** – Drawing pencils are designated by hardness and softness. H pencils are hard and make lighter marks; B pencils are soft and make darker marks. Pencils range from very soft (9B) to very hard (9H). *Recommended:* 2B, HB, and 2H.

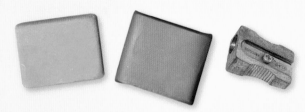

• **Erasers** – Plastic erasers are best for erasing hard pencil marks and large areas. Kneaded erasers can be molded into different shapes and are great for lifting out highlights.

• **Sharpener** – You can achieve various effects depending on how sharp or dull your pencil is, but generally you'll want to keep your pencil sharp at all times.

• **Blending Stumps (also called tortillons)** – Blending stumps allow you to blend or soften lines and small areas of your drawing.

• **Tracing Paper** – Tracing paper allows you to transfer the outlines of your sketch to a fresh sheet of paper. Simply place your sketch on the surface of a light box (an inexpensive tabletop device that lights up inside); then place a sheet of tracing paper on top of the sketch, and turn the light box on. The light box illuminates the sketch underneath so that you can trace over it, thereby transferring the lines of your drawing. You can also create your own "light box" by placing a lamp under a glass table or using a window flooded with natural light.

Optional supplies – A ruler or T-square to mark the perimeter of your drawing, artist's tape to attach your paper to your drawing surface, and paintbrushes and a mixing palette if you use paints. (See "Color Mediums," page 9.)

Drawing Basics

Basic Pencil Techniques

The basic pencil techniques below can help you render everything from smooth hair to rough wood. Feel free to experiment and try new techniques, but always apply shading evenly in a back-and-forth motion over the same area.

Hatching This technique consists of a series of parallel strokes. The closer the strokes, the darker the tone will be.

Crosshatching For darker shading, layer parallel strokes on top of one another at varying angles.

Shading Darkly Apply heavy pressure to the pencil to create dark, linear areas of shading.

Gradating Apply heavy pressure with the side of your pencil, gradually lightening as you go.

Creating Form

Any subject can be broken down into variations of three basic shapes: a circle, square, and triangle.

Adding a few lines gives the shapes depth.

Adding a bit of shading gives the shapes form.

Identifying Values

Shading objects creates contrasts in *value* (the lightness or darkness of black or a color). When shading a subject, consider the light source—this is what determines the placement of highlights and shadows. The *highlight* (lightest value) is where the light source directly strikes the object. The gray area between the highlight and the shadow is the actual color of the object. The *cast shadow* is the shadow cast onto the ground by the object. The *form shadow* is the shadow on the object itself. *Reflected light* bounces up from the surface and strikes the object.

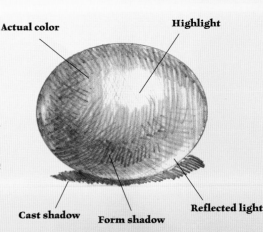

Actual color

Highlight

Cast shadow

Form shadow

Reflected light

Color Basics

Color can help bring your drawings to life, but first it helps to know a bit about color theory. There are three *primary* colors: red, yellow, and blue. These colors cannot be created by mixing other colors. Mixing two primary colors produces a *secondary* color: orange, green, and purple. Mixing a primary color with a secondary color produces a *tertiary* color: red-orange, red-purple, yellow-orange, yellow-green, blue-green, and blue-purple. Reds, yellows, and oranges are "warm" colors; greens, blues, and purples are "cool" colors. See the color combinations below for more mixing ideas.

The Color Wheel

A color wheel is useful for understanding relationships between colors. Knowing where each color is located on the color wheel makes it easy to understand how colors relate to and react with one another.

Easy Color Combinations

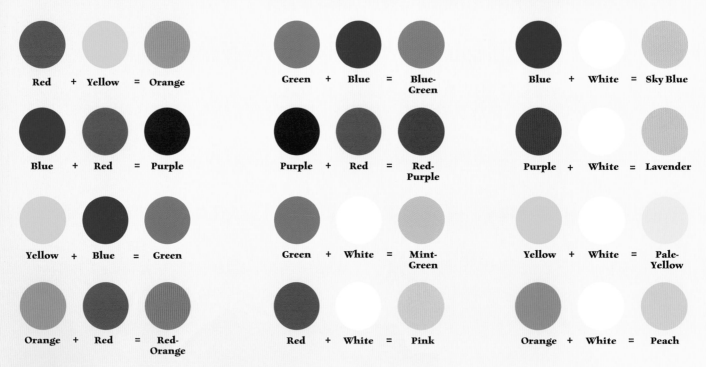

Red + Yellow = Orange	Green + Blue = Blue-Green	Blue + White = Sky Blue
Blue + Red = Purple	Purple + Red = Red-Purple	Purple + White = Lavender
Yellow + Blue = Green	Green + White = Mint-Green	Yellow + White = Pale-Yellow
Orange + Red = Red-Orange	Red + White = Pink	Orange + White = Peach

Adding Color to Your Drawing

Some artists draw directly on illustration board or watercolor paper and then apply color directly to the original pencil drawing; however, if you are a beginning artist, you might opt to preserve your original pencil drawing by making several photocopies and applying color to a photocopy. This way, you'll always have your original drawing in case you make a mistake or you want to experiment with different colors or mediums.

Color Media

Colored Pencils

Colored pencils are a convenient and easy method for applying color on virtually any paper surface. To create blends with colored pencils, simply layer colors on top of one another.

Art Markers

Alcohol-based art markers offer a nice finish when applied to photocopies, but make sure that the photocopy toner is dry before applying color. Markers and colored pencils may also be used in combination with paints to further enhance and accent your drawings.

Watercolor Paint

To paint your photocopied drawing in watercolor, mount the photocopy onto a two-ply, plate-finish illustration board or Bristol board. You can use a ready-made adhesive board to secure your photocopied paper, or you can apply a spray adhesive to the board (make sure that you do this in a well-ventilated area) and then adhere your photocopy. Make sure that there are no air bubbles between the photocopy and the board, or the paper will curl when wet media is applied. Allow the paper to dry before applying watercolor.

Acrylic Paint

To work with acrylic paint, place your photocopied drawing onto a Masonite board using a diluted coat of acrylic gesso. Mix equal parts gesso and water; then use a large brush to generously apply the mixture over both the board and the photocopy. Remove air bubbles between the photocopy and the board. Allow the gesso to dry completely. Work by layering your color in thin glazes or washes, building up the color and intensity. After your washes have dried, you can use thicker, less diluted acrylic paint for details or to create an opaque quality.

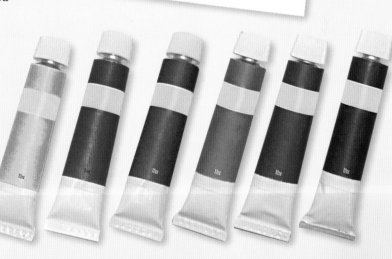

A Note about Digital Painting

The illustrations in this book were drawn in graphite pencil and then colored digitally using a pen tablet and image-manipulation software. Working digitally allows you to experiment with a variety of methods without losing your original artwork; however, you don't need to paint digitally to create beautiful color artwork. Markers, watercolors, acrylics, and colored pencils are all fantastic mediums. In fact, many of the same color effects you see in this book can be created using these tools.

CHAPTER 2

Magical Creatures

Legends and books often take us into a land of imagination, where almost anything can happen. A page turns and there you are, face to face with unbelievable creatures whose special gifts make them different from anyone—or anything—you've ever met. Some of them can harness the forces of nature, chasing away rain clouds just in time for a special event. Some of them have supernatural strength, perfect for battling bad guys. Some of them have bodies covered with scales, making them invincible to warrior's blades so they can guard a valuable treasure.

While other people may not believe in dwarves or elves or gargoyles, there's something about these strange creatures that rings true. For centuries, legends have been told all around the world about beings with magical abilities. Pegasus, a flying horse, descends from ancient Greek mythology, but he's still popular today in video games and

movies. (And he'd make a great pet—imagine riding him to school or over to your best friend's house!)

Likewise, stories of elves have been told around campfires in Germany, Scandinavia, England, and Ireland. Sometimes these elves are tall, magical, and beautiful; sometimes they're tiny and full of mischief. They've been blamed for tying knots in people's hair while they sleep and for making farm animals sick by shooting arrows at them. Think about how one of these little creatures could spice up your history class if you hid one in your pocket. Now that would be cool!

In the British Isles, tales of magical sea creatures—half-human, half-fish—have been told since the days of the ancient Celts. Mermaids took the form of human women and appeared on land during fairs, looking for men to marry—an act that would give them a soul. Some people believed that mermaids could grant wishes; others believed that they lured men to their death by drowning. Either way, you might want to think twice before inviting a half-human, half-fish person into your boat the next time you go fishing. After all, these aren't the watered-down (pun intended), joyfully singing, red-haired mermaids seen in cartoons.

This chapter is filled with all sorts of magical characters. So go ahead, turn the page and dive in.

Mermaid

Lately, everybody and their sister wishes they could sing—just like our mermaid, who dreams of one day becoming a siren. She told her parents that she was going to sun herself on the rocks. Instead, she's trying to convince those sailors that her singing skills are legendary.

Step One Using an HB pencil, sketch a centerline and gesture lines to indicate the arms. Notice how the centerline of the torso suggests a leaning position and slight twist of the spine. Then add simple sketch lines to indicate the pelvis and shoulders. Draw a cylinder for the neck to add volume. Then draw her head in the shape of a skull. Because her tail is a soft form, be sure to draw it as a curving, free-flowing shape. This mermaid should have a fluid, feminine appearance.

Step Two Add cylindrical form to the arms to add volume and define the proportions. With this framework in place, you are now ready to sketch in the anatomical details.

⁜ T I P ⁜ Start with simple shapes and build your drawing from there. Notice how the top of the mermaid's pelvis looks like swimming trunks. Drawing can be easier when you break figures down into simple shapes.

Step Three Sketch in the rough figure details and add shape to her head; then begin drawing in strands of hair. Draw in the rock beneath her, as well as the seascape around her.

Step Four Sketch in the rough shape of legs and add more definition to the fish tail. Note the angle where her knees would be (if she had them). Add detail to her hands and the rock, and further develop her hair.

13

Step Five Continue refining her face and hair, and add gill slits to her neck. Add detail to the fins along her forearms.

Step Six Refine the underlying structure of the face and lighten her eyebrows. Add more shadow to her figure, noting where the shadow of her left arm falls over her hips. Continue enhancing the scales, and use a kneaded eraser to lift out a highlight running the length of her tail. Use a darker 2B pencil to further enhance the line work.

Siren or Mermaid?

Have you ever wondered if your classmate might be a siren or a mermaid? Unfortunately, no final exams are going to reveal her secrets. If she is a mythical creature pretending to be human, you're going to need the skills of a sleuth to discover the truth. Below are 10 tips for uncovering which of these legendary beauties dwells among your crowd.

1. She always wears long dresses so you never see her legs.

2. She's won the school talent contest five years in a row.

3. Sushi is her favorite food.

4. When she sings, she can convince all of her teachers to give easy tests.

5. She can hold her breath underwater for extended periods of time.

6. Her brother puts wax in his ears when she asks to borrow his car.

7. She can swim faster than an Olympic gold medalist.

8. She loves to play the harp.

9. She's never going to get the hang of walking in high heels.

10. If she starts to hum in class, none of the boys will pay attention to the teacher.

Answers:

She's a Mermaid if 1, 3, 5, 7, and 9 are true.

She's a Siren if 2, 4, 6, 8, and 10 are true.

Step Seven Finish drawing in the background details using an HB pencil, and add splashes and foam to the water.

Capturing Details

Notice the spiny fins that run the length of the mermaid's forearms, as well as the webbing between her fingers. These details make her look well-adapted to ocean swimming.

Based on a swordfish tail, the mermaid's tail consists of an overarching outer supporting spine and inner, more flexible webbing and spines. This is repeated on the small dorsal fin on her tail and the fins on her forearms.

Step Eight A variety of effects are used to portray the ocean. Various shades of dark green indicate the troughs between the higher waves, light blue helps show reflected light on the water's surface, and blue-green works well for the waves and foam. For the jagged rocks, use gray and red- or green-browns. Dark blue-gray helps indicate shadows, and light blue adds shine to the tail. Finally, red-orange in the sky signifies danger for the crippled ship.

Elf

Some elves rule Middle Earth, while others rule the local forest. Often confused with fairies, pixies, and brownies, elves sometimes act like the bratty kid on the playground. They'll steal your lunch, tie your shoelaces together, and hide your homework. But if you're lucky enough to befriend an elf, he might just teach you how to make yourself invisible the next time your math teacher calls on you.

Step One Use an HB pencil to rough out a stick figure with circles at the joints. Draw in some construction lines on the head to map out the placement of the eyes and the nose; then rough in the ears.

Step Two Begin to rough in the elf's anatomy. Sketch some shaggy hair and rough facial features. Situate the elf in the scene by indicating the ground beneath his feet.

Step Three Now refine the placement of the elf's face and muscles. Using a kneaded eraser, remove some of the old sketch lines from steps one and two.

Step Four Here I adjusted the elf's right hand to a lower position for a more natural pose. Use a kneaded eraser in a tapping motion to gently lighten the underlying illustration and remove old sketch lines. Begin to sketch in the elf's costume and refine his face a bit more. Lightly sketch in some background details, including a root and a caterpillar.

Step Five Tighten up the elf's costume and flint weapon, using a darker HB pencil to further refine the details.

Step Six Begin using shading to emphasize the volume of the figure's limbs. Shade in the elf's face, creating a strongly delineated shadow beneath his chin.

Step Seven Continue to layer in the details using a combination of crosshatching and soft shading. Draw in heavy outlines to build up the background foliage and caterpillar, adding shading to these elements as well.

Step Eight Use a kneaded eraser to clean up any old sketch lines and to finish lifting out the highlights on the elf's figure. Finally, darken up the figure's outlines using a 2B pencil.

Step Nine This palette consists of greens, yellows, gray, and a few subtle earth tones. The elf's tunic is a velvety shade of pea green, and his tights are gray-green. The shadows are infused with saturated blues, blue-greens, violets, and purples. Use various earth tones to create a convincing appearance for the ground and background highlights.

Gargoyle

This gargoyle has grown weary of his normal occupation guarding a medieval cathedral from evil spirits. He perches on a ledge in the midst of transforming from stone to living flesh. He's watching as tourists wander past, wondering if any of them have candy in their pockets or backpacks. Keep this in mind the next time you're tempted to eat sweets between meals.

Step One Draw a loose figure outline, using circles to denote the joints. Rough in the areas where the facial features will go.

Step Two Continue to rough in the body, making it more anatomical. Erase underlying sketch lines to help clarify the pose. Begin detailing the gargoyle's left hand to reinforce a rigid pose.

{ TIP } *Try experimenting with different wing positions and sizes.*

Step Three Continue adding detail to the face, wings, and hands. Then layer in sketch lines to clearly indicate the muscles. Darken the figure's outlines, and add a bit of dark shading to the veins that appear on the right hand and leg—the "living" side.

Step Four Erase unnecessary sketch lines, and continue to firm up the outer line work. Shade the bottom part of the wing and add deep shade-defining shadows to the "stone" side of the gargoyle. Experiment using some of the pencil techniques discussed on page 7 to further define the forms and enhance the stone-like look. Use your finger to soften the shading on the living side of the gargoyle, and darken the stone side so it has a harder edge.

Step Five Continue building up the inner volumes with shading, and further define the extremities and face. Then add shading just below the knuckles of the right hand so that it looks as if it's pressing down and creating an impression on the right leg. Use your finger to soften some edges on the living side of the gargoyle. Add stippling—a series of small dots—to the stone side, as well as some fine "cracks" to emphasize the feel of weathered cement. Use light crosshatching to add extra gray to the stone side. Finally, darken the figure's outline with a 2B pencil.

Step Six Now add a realistic background. This gnarly guy is right at home on a lofty perch. So draw him on the side of an old stone cathedral, complete with medieval statuary and a rainy, windswept European village in the distance.

Step Seven This predominantly gray color scheme accentuates the cold stone of the cathedral and the oppressive mood of the Dark Ages. It also contrasts nicely against the side of the gargoyle that is slowly coming to life, which is rendered in warm ochre: a shade of golden orange. Use a touch of orange for the village lights that shine below. Add touches of purple and light magenta to further complement the ochre. Finally, use light blue for the rain.

Pegasus

The ultimate dream ride, this mythical winged horse could take you just about anywhere—that is, if you were clever enough to steal him away from Bellerophon, the Greek hero who rode him into battle. According to legend, this flying horse called Pegasus had a stellar ending, for he was later transformed into a constellation by Zeus. In this drawing, Pegasus soars high above the clouds, wings spread wide. Wild and untamed, he looks like he has enough energy to circle the sun.

Step One Sketch a gestural drawing to capture the overall pose using circles to denote the joints in the front and hind legs. Use ovals to identify the largest masses in Pegasus's physique; then block out the general shape of the wings.

Step Two Use a light pencil to begin adding detail. Work loosely filling in muscle structure and Pegasus's head, noting the dynamic play of muscles. Work in the feathers on his wings.

26

Step Three Begin to darken the outline, and continue to refine the underlying skeletal structure and musculature.

❋ TIP ❋ Pegasus's body structure is virtually identical to that of a horse. Keep this in mind as you sketch so that your drawing is both believable and interesting.

Step Four Add more shading to bring out the various planes and volumes of the anatomy. Note the strong planes on the neck and the cylindrical volume defined by the abdomen. Begin to firm up the definition of the feathers on the wings.

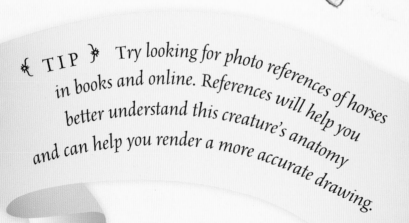

❊ TIP ❊ Try looking for photo references of horses in books and online. References will help you better understand this creature's anatomy and can help you render a more accurate drawing.

Step Five Here I slightly adjusted Pegasus's front left leg for better accuracy. Continue crosshatching and shading; defining muscles; and refining details, such as the hair and feathery texture of the wings. Use your finger to soften the lines and enhance the shading.

Step Six Darken the outlines to help create the illusion of volume and space. Use a kneaded eraser to lift out highlights and to clean up your underlying sketch. Use your fingertips to soften some of the detail on Pegasus's ribs to make him look more robust.

Step Seven This scene has a vibrant color palette consisting of white, magenta, purple, and a bit of gray for Pegasus's body. Orange, yellow, pink, and violet fill this sky.

Warrior

This Japanese warrior wears Samurai armor and is ready to go into battle. Lithe, lean, and probably mean, this guy could convince the biggest bully at school to clean up his room—immediately. Brandishing a long sword and wearing traditional Samurai warrior arm and shin guards, this character depicts a dramatic pose—a classic stance seen in many martial arts films. It might not be the best fighting position, but it sure looks cool!

Step One Sketch a stick figure, using circles to indicate the joints and simple shapes to indicate the body mass.

Step Two Begin developing the underlying anatomy. Sketch in faint facial detail, and refine the outline and position of the warrior's hands.

Step Three Continue to build up the head and face. Sketch the armor plates using simple shapes. Feel free to use historical references to render this warrior as accurately as possible. Erase unnecessary sketch lines before continuing.

Step Four Fill in more detail on the warrior's armor. Tighten up the face and hands, and block out more of the armor plating. Use a visual reference of Samurai armor to help create the warrior's costume.

Step Five Samurai armor is constructed of small overlapping metal plates tied together with cord. Begin to detail the armor and weapons using an HB pencil, and tighten the detail of the character's shoulder protectors (called *sode*) to make them more historically accurate.

Step Six Give this warrior a grim and determined look with a well-defined battle scar running down his right cheek. Then begin shading his hair and select areas of his armor.

Step Seven Shade the design on the warrior's tunic and render reflection details on his arm guards (*kote*) and shin guards (*suneate*). Add more detail and darker values to his hair; then gently shade the figure overall to reveal some internal volume. Finally, use a kneaded eraser to remove unnecessary sketch lines.

Step Eight Genuine samurai armor can be quite colorful. This palette consists of various yellows, golds, blues, purples, greens, reds, and browns. A touch of light blue helps emphasize the side lighting on the face.

Dragon

You may feel like you can breathe fire after eating one of your mom's spicy enchiladas, but this scaly guy could turn you into toast with a single puff. With massive wings, claw-studded arms, and an armor-plated body, the dragon has spawned legends and myths for thousands of years. And right now, this guy would like you to keep on believing that he's imaginary so you won't even *dream* about stealing his treasure. Forearm raised, claws extended, and steam sizzling, this dragon poses in a defensive stance, ready to fight anyone who looks even slightly interested in his swag.

Step One Using light strokes, rough out the dragon's graceful yet powerful mass. Map out the joints with simple lines and circles. Note that the indication for the neck and spine are S shaped, while the body and limbs are thick. Block in a rough indication of heavy brow ridges, a solid snout, and bat-like wings.

Step Two Begin building up muscle and roughing in scales. Draw in the bony structure of the wings, including a hook-like detail at the thumb joint—at the top of the wing—similar to the climbing hooks bats have on their wings. Add pointy scales along the spine, dinosaur-like claws, and spikes to the dragon's forearms. Sketch in the eyes and sharp teeth.

Step Three Start refining the wings and adding scales to the body and face. Draw pointy projections on the creature's face and to the top of the brow ridges. Add a beard hanging off the end of the chin. Next, draw in some muscular details in the shoulder and hips. This is a fire-breathing dragon, so create a thin column of smoke drifting out of his mouth. Continue to layer in more facial details.

Step Four Darken the outlines to define the dragon's form. Continue to add detail to the scales and muscles. This dragon is an intelligent being, so give it human-like eyes. This unexpected element will make him look even more dangerous.

❈ TIP ❉
Note that the dragon's nose is similar in shape to the flukes on a whale's tail.

Step Five Add shadows under the chin
and belly for dimension. To make the
wings appear translucent, draw a lightly
shaded tail that shows through the right
wing membrane.

Step Six Darken the outlines with
a 2B pencil to bring out the form and
dimension.

Step Seven Color the dragon with purples and blues, using bright red for dramatic side lighting. Use a yellow-gold for the background to further complement the dragon's color. Color the interior of the cave with a variety of browns, gray, greens, and purples. Create detail in the treasure by using a variety of yellows, golds, and oranges.

Dwarf

This burly guy with an attitude looks like he could single-handedly steal your lunch money and then break into your locker. No worries—your secret stash of jawbreakers is safe. This dwarf warrior is most often found between the pages of a book on Norse or Germanic mythology than in your school hallway. Mouth open in an ancient battle cry, shield clutched in one hand and a sword in the other, every muscle of this dwarf warrior is willing and ready to fight.

Step One Block out the figure with simple sketch lines. Stay mindful of the proportions, keeping the head large in relationship to the body. Be sure to give the illusion of movement and weight bearing. Some areas will overlap, such as the arm that holds the shield.

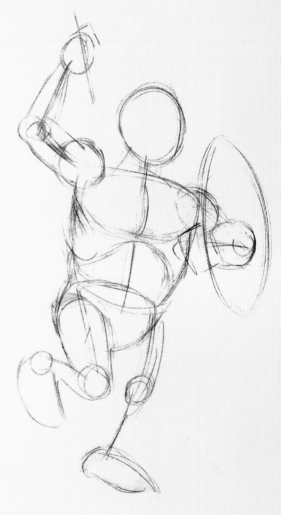

Step Two Rough in the basic musculature, paying attention to how the muscles flex. Sketch guidelines for the facial features.

Step Three Once you are satisfied with your sketch, lightly rough in the details of the costume and armaments. Erase unnecessary pencil marks.

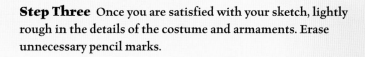

❮ TIP ❯
Consult photos of medieval armor and weaponry to help you capture the intricate details.

Step Four Now refine the intricate details of the costume. Note the muscles and tendons in the raised arm and the scar on the face. Add shading to further define the beard and facial hair.

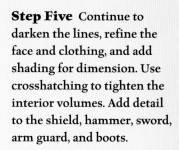

Step Five Continue to
darken the lines, refine the
face and clothing, and add
shading for dimension. Use
crosshatching to tighten the
interior volumes. Add detail
to the shield, hammer, sword,
arm guard, and boots.

Step Six For this diminutive warrior with a flaming red beard, use earth tones, fiery oranges, and brilliant yellows for your basic palette. Complement these colors with purples and blue-grays. The various metal objects of his costume should be rendered with a lot of shine using colors that suggest rust, dirt, and tarnish. An effective use of silhouette helps create the feel of a vicious war raging in the background.

Witch

Maybe she's conjuring up monsters to inhabit your nightmares, or maybe she's unleashing demons to protect you from the neighborhood ninja-wannabes. However you look at it, this witch stands poised and ready to cast a spell of epic proportions. With candles and incense burning, one hand holding a snake and the other clutching a skull-crested dagger, this character combines elements of earthly beauty and fearful power. In this dramatic pose there exists a strong contrast between dark and light—an eerie light source comes from below.

Step One Rough in the body masses, including the head, chest, and hips. Note the proportions to ensure that the figure has an appropriate sense of weight and balance.

Step Two Now draw the headpiece, flowing hair, and cape, as well as an indication of the "magic circle" beneath her and the column of smoke rising behind her. Erase unneeded sketch lines.

Step Three Erase sketch lines that you no longer need. Add the armbands, dress bindings, sandal lacings, and scabbard for her ceremonial dagger.

Step Four Build up the muscle detail in her arms and leg to add tension and a sense of physical power to the pose.

Step Five Use shading to establish how the light plays across her form. The light source should appear to come from below, thus enhancing the supernatural feel of the illustration. Begin outlining the form with dark, heavy lines.

Step Six Continue to add darker, heavier shading and more value to the blacks. Build up the smoke billowing out around her.

Step Seven Darken the shading, and lift out faint highlights from the straps on her gown. Blend the hair, and soften the shading on her leg around the knee. Lift out some highlights on her face, and darken the details around the eyes and mouth. Add denizens from a mystical dimension—all of them transforming from the magic smoke. Note that I removed the heel on the left shoe in this step to keep the costume authentic.

Step Eight This palette consists of purples, blues, greens, and yellows. Color the creatures in the smoke dark purple, rendering their eyes in hot pink. Use the same colors in the palette to render the witch's skin, which reflects the colors and light surrounding her. Add light highlights to shiny objects, such as the jewelry, dagger, and "pet" snake.

CHAPTER 3

Mythological Creatures

For thousands of years, myths have been told and retold. They've been chanted around flickering campfires, whispered in shadowy forests, and even told as bedtime stories. In many ways, myths resemble the rumors you hear at lunch—like the weird stories about what your classmates did over summer vacation. There are several key differences, however, between a myth and a rumor. It doesn't matter, for example, whether a myth is true or not; quite often these tales are considered sacred. But the most important difference is probably the fact that myths speak about the adventures of gods and creatures that possess supernatural abilities. These are the creatures that rise from the mists of the ancient past when these stories are told.

With hair made of writhing snakes and a face that could turn you to stone if you looked upon it, Medusa was once a Gorgon. The original queen of the "bad-hair day," she was turned into a monstrous beast by the goddess Athena. Unfortunately, Medusa was a mortal and therefore Perseus was able to kill her by cutting off her head. We learn of her exploits from Greek mythology.

The stories of Grendel come from the epic poem *Beowulf,* written between the 8th and 11th centuries. Although penned by an Anglo-Saxon, the story itself does not take place in Britain, but rather in Denmark. Here, a vicious dragon-like monster lived in the swamps, and he couldn't stand to listen to the people who sang, danced, and celebrated in the king's mead hall. (Obviously, this monster didn't know how to have a good time.) He would continually attack the king's hall and kill all the revelers. That is, until a warrior named Beowulf came into town. And the rest, as they say, is history.

A third mythological creature was born in the Greek isle of ancient Crete. Set amid Mediterranean seas, this tiny island kingdom contained a dangerous underground labyrinth. A half-human, half-bull creature called a Minotaur lived here. He would feed upon humans—sacrifices who had been set loose in the maze. In this myth, an Athenian named Theseus killed the Minotaur. This Greek hero was able to find his way out of the maze by following a ball of red twine: Ancient Greece's version of a GPS system.

Stories of these strange, super-natural creatures have been told for centuries. Now, with just a turn of the page, you too can enter into the world of ancient mythology. Here you will also learn the secrets necessary to capture and tame these beasts with pencil and paper.

Minotaur

Known for prowling a deadly maze in ancient Minoan Crete, this half-man, half-bull creature played a mean game of hide-and-seek in his day. The latest rumor is that he poses like this five days a week down at the local mall. Apparently, shoplifting has dropped 87 percent since his arrival at the main kiosk. This Minotaur poses with a huge wooden mallet in hand, ready to deliver a deathblow to some poor ancient Greek adventurer.

Step One Establish the spine and the position of the arms, legs, and hips in an action pose. Then rough in the body mass.

Step Two Sketch in contour lines for the muscles, and add definition to the fingers and the hooves.

Step Three Rough in more detail on the Minotaur's abdomen, chest, and leg muscles, concentrating on capturing the stretch and tension of these muscle groups in motion. Sketch in the details of the face and head. Erase unnecessary sketch lines.

{ TIP } *Placement of the spine, hips, and chest are important when drawing a convincing humanoid figure.*

Step Four Continue to refine the muscle details. Notice how the bulging leg muscles, as well as the positions of the loincloth, tail, and broken chain on his wrist emphasize the speed and power of his movement. Note that I slightly adjusted the position of the left hand to make it look more powerful.

Step Five Start to build up final shading using shadows to refine the Minotaur's physique. Pay attention to details, such as the veins, tendons, and striations in the muscles. Add light feathered hatching with an HB pencil, and use your fingers to blend the shading for a softer effect.

Step Six Use shading and short linear strokes to help create the texture of the fur on his leg. Outline the major forms of the Minotaur's legs; then use softer shading to refine their form.

Step Seven Gently tap a kneaded eraser over the sketch lines you want to eliminate. Use a kneaded eraser to introduce highlights in areas on his muscles, horns, eyes, and teeth.

Step Eight The primary color palette for the Minotaur includes variations of yellow ochre, brown, and purple. Add a bit of purple in the ochre and brown tones for the body. There are also small hints of green, red, and blue throughout the body.

Grendel

This beast looks like he was spawned in one of your own worst nightmares. Infamous for terrorizing the mead hall of an ancient Viking king, Grendel crouches, ready to finish off an armor-clad warrior like a mid-morning snack. Grendel's breath alone could have probably knocked this opponent unconscious. This hulking beast is a mass of raw muscle, spiny claws, and dagger-like teeth, all poised and ready to put an end to the Viking soldier who plagues him. Meanwhile, somewhere nearby, another Viking stands ready to take on this monster—none other than the mighty Beowulf.

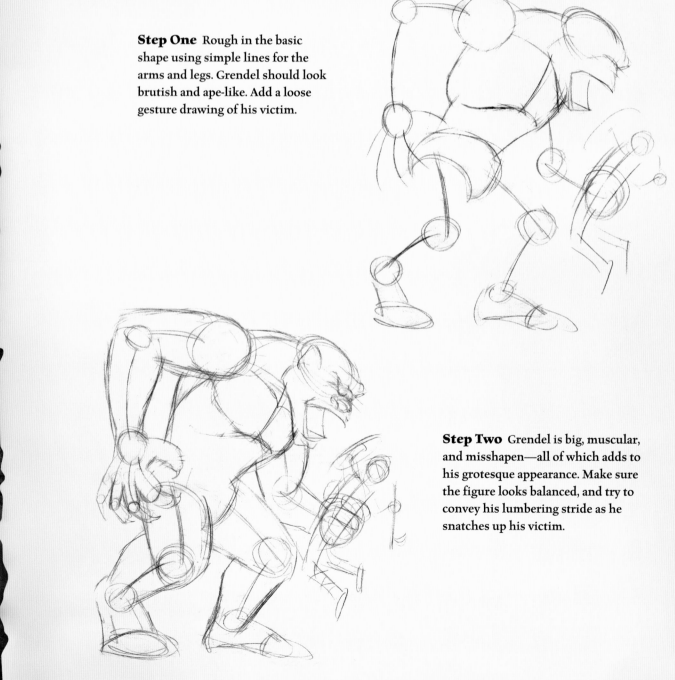

Step One Rough in the basic shape using simple lines for the arms and legs. Grendel should look brutish and ape-like. Add a loose gesture drawing of his victim.

Step Two Grendel is big, muscular, and misshapen—all of which adds to his grotesque appearance. Make sure the figure looks balanced, and try to convey his lumbering stride as he snatches up his victim.

Step Three Now rough in some muscles, and begin adding facial details.

Step Four Continue adding the details that make this monster particularly disturbing: an oversized mouth filled with jagged fangs; a long arm, massive hand, and thick legs; an extremely thick neck; veins, spikes, and odd spiny growths; and warts all over.

Step Five Start tightening the detail of his right arm and loincloth. Then focus on the shadow side of his veins. Note that Grendel's nose has changed here to play up the fact that he is a cave-dwelling creature with a bat-like nose to match his ears. Refine the spiny growths so they appear to be piercing his flesh. Darken the outlines of the forms, keeping the lines fluid.

Step Six Add more detail to Grendel's face, neck, and right hand. Draw in more shadows under his arm and chin to help establish his solidity. Continue to darken the outlines.

Step Seven Shade Grendel's body and begin adding more detail to the Viking. Notice the cast shadow from Grendel's right arm, which appears on his right thigh.

Step Eight Finalize the line work and continue to darken the heavily shadowed areas on both Grendel and the Viking. Continue to add striations to Grendel's straining muscles. Render the warts and veins that protrude from his body. Add wrinkles, more veins, and soft shading where appropriate. Give a wilder look to his one visible eye so that he now looks like a raging monster—which is exactly what we want!

Step Nine Now use a softer, darker 2B pencil to punch up your line work and further deepen the shadows. Use your fingers to soften the values of the shading. Finally, use a kneaded eraser to lift out highlights and clean up old sketch lines. You've got yourself one mean monster there!

Step Ten This limited color palette is meant to evoke fire and night. The red-orange colors on the left side of the frame suggest danger. The cool blue in the background evokes the Frozen North where the story takes place. Use an interplay of orange and blue to help further define the figures and add drama to this scene.

Isis

Isis, an ancient Egyptian goddess who was considered a perfect mother, is shown here soaring through the skies. Also known as a friend to the downtrodden, she might be sailing over the local school right now, watching hoards of teens like a dedicated but nosy hall monitor. Now is not the time to get in a fight with your friends over who among you has the best cell phone. Usually depicted standing still, this drawing of Isis is shown flying—a dynamic pose that demonstrates her magical qualities.

Step One Sketch the basic pose of Isis using a light pencil. Add a contour line down the length of the body, and sketch in the wings and arms.

Step Two Begin building up the volumes. Add more detail to the wings, which reflect Egyptian style. Lightly sketch in the headdress, as well as the staff in her right hand.

Step Three Begin drawing in the clothing details. Isis's staff and headdress contain a stylized symbol of the sun, which is supported by cow horns. The ankh on her belt is a symbol of eternal life in Egyptian art.

Step Four Use curved lines to fully capture the contours of the figure and clothes. Make sure to draw the elements *through* the sketch so they appear to wrap around each other. Details like the armbands convey depth and dimension.

Step Five Continue to refine your lines and erase unnecessary sketch marks. Begin darkening the outline of the wings. Isis's costume is shiny, so lift out highlights on the headdress, bodice, and shirt to emphasize this effect. The shadow under Isis's chin establishes that the light source is coming from slightly above and shining down on her face and figure.

Step Six Continue shading, noting
how the value on the underside of
the wings adds dimension and brings
the figure forward. Lightly shade
the head of the staff, and add some
light lines to show how it emanates a
mysterious and mystical light.

Step Seven Punch up some of
the line work and details with a
darker 2B lead. Finally, add a rich
black outline around her wings—
which have been blended—for a
graphic look.

Step Eight Isis's costume is gold and green, symbolizing royalty. Keep the color palette simple, using hints of purple to shade her skin and darker values of golden brown on her costume. Add highlights with light yellow. Fill the background with light blue-green, purple, pink, and yellow.

Satyr

Half-goat, half-human, the satyr danced and drank his way through Greek mythology. He enjoyed frolicking through the woods and was a frequent sidekick of the gods, Dionysus and Pan. He is often depicted playing music on a panpipe: an instrument made from hollow reeds. Just like he's dancing a jig, this mischievous satyr jumps from one foot to the other as he plays a cheery song.

Step One Use simple lines to rough in the pose.

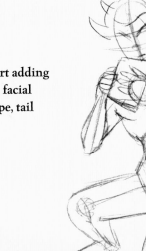

Step Two Start adding the horns, ears, facial features, panpipe, tail and hooves.

Step Three Continue to build up and refine the muscles.

Step Four Start adding darker pencil lines and shading. Use crosshatching to indicate the various planes of the body that you want to shade with darker values. Begin to incorporate more goat-like features into the face, particularly the nose and eyes.

Step Five Continue to outline the satyr with darker, thicker lines. Simplify and refine the line work and anatomy as you draw, and work on the facial details. Add a slight goatee, and slightly refine the position of the lips to make it look like he's blowing into the pipes. Tighten the subtle play of veins over the tendons in his arms by lifting out faint highlights and adding shading around their edges. Slightly adjust the satyr's raised foot by giving it a small break at the joint right over the hoof.

Step Six Continue refining the outline and shading, using circular strokes to create the look of wool.

Step Seven Continue layering in circular strokes to create the wool texture. Lift out select areas to add highlights that show where the light source is coming from. Lightly sketch in a mountain behind the satyr.

Step Eight Lightly sketch over the wool with a soft lead and smudge a bit with your finger. Use a kneaded eraser to lift out highlights on the arms, face, and torso. Complete the shadow he casts on the ground.

Step Nine The satyr lives in pastoral woods and mountains; therefore, the outdoor color palette should include green and blue. Use earth tones for the his skin and fur, punctuated by dark blue outlines for dimension.

Sphinx

This enigmatic sphinx perches on a rock, looking for someone to test. Strewn on the ground below her are the remains of past warriors and travelers who failed to answer her riddle. Neither armor nor swords were able to protect them if they answered incorrectly. (Just be glad your history teacher doesn't grade tests like this!) This sphinx combines the scary elements of a lion, an eagle, and a human—and she looks ready to pounce at any moment.

Step One Use simple lines to block in the shapes, paying attention to the creature's proportions. Rough in the rock beneath the sphinx.

Step Two Now rough out the human head, thick hair, and bird-like wings. Add a bit of detail to the claws and face. Add guidelines for the feathers on the wings. Use a kneaded eraser to clean up old sketch lines.

Step Three The sphinx is powerful, frightening, and muscular—like a killer cat. Define the snarl on her face and block in the rows of feathers on her wings. Refine the front and hind legs. Sketch in some of the leftovers from her past meals at the base of the rock. Add shading to better define the body mass and fur texture.

Step Four Begin refining the outlines of the figure, and add shading to the front legs and claws. Start tightening the detail of the mane and face.

Step Five Use a softer 2B pencil to darken the shading on the underside of the wing, as well as the shadow that the wing casts on her body. Continue to add shading on the face, body, and hair using very fine crosshatching strokes; then use your finger to soften it. Add strokes over the shading to create the texture of fur.

Step Six Refine and tighten the details of the remains that lay strewn below her. Keep the crosshatching strokes on the stone crisp to help give the rock a rough, solid texture. Add more tone to her hair, face, and body; then punch up the value of the shading under the wings, on her body, and on the ground. Finally, use a kneaded eraser to clean up unwanted lines and to lift out subtle highlights in her hair, back, and limbs.

Step Seven A light green sky emphasizes the otherworld quality of the sphinx. The rest of the color palette evokes the dusty, sun-baked landscape of ancient Greece. Render an occasional shadow in blue-purple to complement the predominantly orange and brown tones. Base the sphinx's color scheme on big predatory cats—the tan coloring of a lion combined with the spots of a leopard.

Zeus

Everybody needs to practice if they want to get their game on—even Zeus. Hailed as the king of the ancient Greek gods, here we see him depicted as a young god, studying the craft that would make him famous. At an age when you might have been practicing video games or perfecting a sport, this young Olympian studied the fine art of throwing lightning bolts. Zeus is usually shown as an older god, with a long flowing beard. But here he is still young, strong, and full of both thunder and lightning.

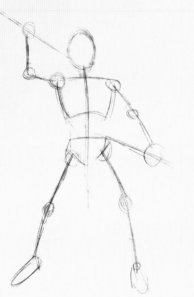

Step One Sketch Zeus in a fairly simple pose. Use simplified lines and shapes for the head, chest, and hips; then use simple circular sketches to rough in the position of the joints. Add a loose suggestion of the lightning bolts, which will help you position his arms and hands.

Step Two Now begin to fill in the volume, blocking out the masses of the limbs and torso. Add simple suggestions of the muscle contours and rough in the structure of the face.

Step Three Continue building up the details of the face and the body, while erasing unnecessary sketch lines. Note the light line that extends from the base of the neck through the spine to the ground. This helps ensure that the character's pose is in balance. The base of the neck should always be positioned over the figure's center of gravity.

Step Four Begin to sketch in the costume, beard, and hair. This version of Zeus has a youthful look with a goatee and a more barbaric hairstyle. Other traditional Greek costume elements include the kilt and sandals. Draw the armbands so they appear to conduct electricity.

Step Five Begin refining the shapes and body mass. Start to add shading around the muscles in his arms to make him appear more realistic. His raised arm should look powerfully rendered, so emphasize the appearance of the veins and tendons under the skin.

Step Six Begin to darken the outline, shading, and electrical current. Then add shading to the cape. Once you've shaded to your liking, use your finger to soften the pencil lines and shadows.

Step Seven Continue to add heavy shading to the cape to create a sense of volume as it whips around in the wind. Refine any other unfinished lines, and use an eraser to get rid of old sketch marks and to introduce highlights in select areas.

Step Eight This primary color palette consists of purple, gold, and blue-purple. Use white for the brilliant lightning bolts, as well as the highlights in his hair. Emphasize the lightning bolts by outlining them in light blue-green. Then dot the sky with a bit of white or gray to suggest stars.

Golem

Mud can be the stuff of nightmares, especially if it causes your soccer team to lose a game. But in ancient Jewish folklore, mud could be used to create a golem: a slow-witted, human-like creature who can't speak. In one 16th-century tale, a rabbi made a golem to protect the Jews in Prague from anti-Semitic attacks. In literature, the golem has given birth to *Frankenstein, The Incredible Hulk*, and a wide variety of monster robots in sci-fi thrillers from the 1950s. In this drawing, the golem lumbers about as a beast of burden, carrying sacks of flour to and fro as commanded.

Step One Start by lightly roughing in the large bulky masses of this creature's body, arms, and legs, as well as the deep-set eyes.

Step Two Further define the form and erase unnecessary sketch lines. Start to suggest the shape of the head.

Step Three Begin adding in details, including the nose and moustache. Draw a face slightly reminiscent of the Moai statues of Easter Island. The golem's head is smaller and disproportionate with the rest of his body, thus giving visual cues that this character is more brawn than brains.

Step Four Draw in lines that suggest his body is formed from rock or clay. The face and body should look powerful, but primitive.

Step Five Using a darker HB pencil, begin darkening the final line work. Note that you're drawing deep fissures in his body, emphasizing that it was crudely made from hand-formed mud. The golem was also used as a servant, so he is shown gingerly carrying bags of flour in his huge arms. Darken his eyes to accent the lack of intelligence in this creature.

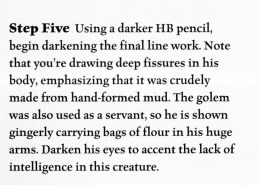

Step Six Now begin to add shading to give the figure better form. You can add dimension by darkening the area on his chest and beneath his chin.

Step Seven Using a 2B pencil, darken the line work and outline. Continue to add shading until you are happy with the result; then use a kneaded eraser to lift out select highlights that emphasize the light source.

Step Eight This subdued palette consists of earthy tan and gray tones. Use blue-gray for the brick building and a light orange for the sky. Use the same blue-gray to add shadows to the golem's clay body.

Medusa

Talk about a bad hair day! While you have all sorts of gel and mousse to get your hair in shape, poor Medusa unwittingly turned every hairdresser in the kingdom to stone. She had to manage and tame her wild snake hair all on her own. This creature from ancient Greek mythology could probably have used a snake charmer as her BFF. This sketch shows Medusa dressed in a traditional Greek gown, with one hand caressing her voluminous head of squirming serpents.

Step One Draw a simple stick figure with developed shapes for the head, upper torso, and hips. One of her hands is shaped like a claw, indicating her predatory nature, while her raised hand strokes the "pets" that grow from her skull.

Step Two Begin to indicate the volume of her body, and sketch a light line from the base of the neck to the ground to ensure that the figure is proportional. Lightly draw in her facial expression.

{ TIP } Always start by drawing a figure's underlying structure—even if it will be draped in clothing. It's a common mistake among beginning artists to draw the clothing before or in place of the body.

Step Three Continue building up the body shape; then start filling in the snakes and elements of her gown. The snakes should look "alive" and writhing, so draw them in different positions. Also start working out how her left hand will interact with her snake hair.

Step Four Continue to layer in more detail. Note the fabric of her gown is light and flowing. Blend shading with your finger to define the contours of her face.

Step Five Start outlining and refining
the contours of her cape and body.

Step Six Darken the
outlines of her dress, cape,
skirt folds, and sandals. Begin
working on the snake details.
Tighten up the claw running
through her hair.

{ TIP } A useful exercise for learning to render fabric and textures is to drape an article of clothing over a piece of furniture. Study the folds, noting the different contours. Take a photo and use it as reference for other drawings.

Slithering Snake Hair

Feel free to detail the snakes' bodies as much or as little as you please. Some snakes look agitated; others appear ready to strike. Notice how they appear to be exploring their surroundings, including wrapping themselves around Medusa's hand and arm. Use your kneaded eraser to lift out highlights in her hair, so the snakes appear realistic.

Step Seven Use an HB pencil to continue shading consistently, noting the direction of the light source. Notice how shadows further define the forms of the drawing.

Step Eight Darken any areas of shading for emphasis, and use your eraser to clean up old sketch lines. Finally, use a 2B pencil to go over the line work, enhance the contours, and emphasize the darkest shadow values.

Step Nine Medusa stands defiantly outside of her cave, with the victims she's turned to stone behind her. Use earthy tones for the background and a combination of light and bright pastel colors for Medusa. A softly colored mauve dress contrasts with the horror of her monstrosity. Color her skin a ghastly green as an outward sign of her cursed life.

CHAPTER 4

Monstrous Creatures

Monsters are the ultimate bad guys. The room always grows quiet when somebody tells a tale about a monster. Even the storyteller's voice drops to a whisper. Go ahead and try it the next time your friends spend the night. Start talking about goblins—real goblins with fierce teeth, hidden lairs, and magical powers. Before long, one of you will get a cold, unexpected shiver. And don't be surprised if you catch your friends glancing over their shoulders when the floor creaks out in the hallway.

Perhaps the most frightening of all monsters is the bogeyman. Maybe this is because you never know where he'll show up—although it's likely to be at night when you're all alone. He could be hiding in your closet or under your bed. He could even be outside your window right now, waiting for you to fall asleep. That's when he'll start scratching on the glass with long, claw-like fingers, hoping that you'll wake up so he can frighten you.

While the bogeyman enjoys scaring children, another monster torments adults. Sometimes called the Angel of Death, the Grim Reaper is often portrayed as a skeleton armed with a nasty-looking scythe. Other times he's shown wearing a black hooded cloak. The scariest part is, you never know when he might turn up. It could be at a party when you're surrounded by friends, at an intersection when you're waiting for the light to turn green, or at the beach when you're waiting for another set of waves. Unfortunately, this monster's mission is always the same: He brings death to those who see him.

The full moon brings this next monster out of hiding. This guy looks and acts perfectly normal for 29 days out of the month—he (or she!) could be your next-door neighbor or your chemistry teacher. Then, on the thirtieth day, a full moon rises and a long, bone-chilling howl echoes through your neighborhood. You might find shreds of a torn shirt and a pair of ripped tennis shoes on the ground surrounded by a combination of human and animal footprints. And that's when you know that a werewolf is on the prowl.

They're all here—the worst monsters you can imagine—from a vampire and swamp creature to the Loch Ness monster. Now turn the page to learn how to draw these elusive beasts. Just remember to leave the light on when you go to sleep!

Vampire

Pizza and soda might sound like a great midnight snack to you, but the tastes of a modern vampire are quite a bit different. This charming bloodsucker takes time to check text messages from a pal back in Romania while waiting for an unsuspecting victim to come strolling past. (Let's hope you're not in his neighborhood right now.) Our vampire is great for learning how to render fabric textures and work with two light sources.

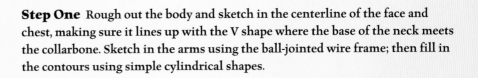

Step One Rough out the body and sketch in the centerline of the face and chest, making sure it lines up with the V shape where the base of the neck meets the collarbone. Sketch in the arms using the ball-jointed wire frame; then fill in the contours using simple cylindrical shapes.

Step Two Sketch in the facial features; then lightly draw in the hair and clothes. Use loose sketch lines to indicate the scarf draping around the vampire's neck. Use your kneaded eraser to lighten up or remove unneeded sketch lines.

Step Three Begin refining the face, adding cat-like pupils and fangs. Darken the contours of the right cheek to further enhance his jaw line, which will mark the edge of the side lighting that you'll add later (See "Side Lighting" on page 97.) Continue to work out the details of his hand and jacket, and lightly sketch skyscrapers and a lamppost in the background.

Step Four Continue to refine and tighten the face, hair, and clothing details. Use dark outlines to create convincing folds in the garments, adding bits of shading in key areas.

Step Five Continue to darken the shading, particularly the clothing creases and shadows around his neck. Use hatching strokes to create texture on the scarf to suggest that it's knitted. Shade in the darkest values of the jacket and his hair, keeping in mind the light that shines from the lamppost and an unseen light source on the figure's right side.

Creating Texture

Creating fabric textures can help show volume and define form. On the upper part of the sleeve, light hatching and selective shading emphasizes the shape of the shoulder. On the lapel, light smudging shows the velvety texture of the jacket against the knitted texture of the scarf, which has been created using small groupings of parallel strokes. Additional hatching on the forearm is built up and smudged in several layers, thereby creating more roundness to the sleeve. Dark outlines tighten and unify the form.

Step Six Continue to shade the darkest areas of the jacket that are facing away from the light source. Shade in the sweater and finish the texture of the scarf. Add some dark shading around the ear, and darken the outline of the hand.

Step Seven Finish shading the vampire's hand, face, and body; then lift out gentle highlights around the shoulder and arm with a kneaded eraser. For a more realistic feel, lift out small highlights on his knuckles and along the veins on his hand. Finish shading the cityscape. With the exception of some lit windows, the thick fog obscures the finer details. Use layer upon layer of shading to fill in the background; then smudge with a blending stump for a slightly blurry look. Add several layers of light shading behind the vampire; then use a kneaded eraser to create the billowy edges of the fog.

Step Eight The red-orange lights of a contemporary urban environment set the mood and provide an excellent palette for this subject. In working with a monochromatic palette—colors belonging to the same family, but with varying shades and hues—the most dynamic effects are achieved by lightening or darkening key areas and introducing one or two additional colors. Subtle sidelights are gray-green and light blue-gray. The strongest blue value will be the vague glow coming up from the cell phone. A piercing shade of green illuminates the eyes.

Side Lighting

Side lighting in this illustration helps define the vampire's face. To create this effect, add light hatching to the central planes of the face—the areas that receive the least amount light.

When the face is completely shaded, use a kneaded eraser to lift out highlights to create the illusion that the light is narrowly shining on him from the side.

Frankenstein's Monster

Like a crazy patchwork quilt, Frankenstein's monster was stitched together using a variety of arms, legs, and fingers from different dead bodies. Because of his strange appearance, he was feared and hated by the local villagers. One of the best literary examples of a loner and an outcast, this character brings new meaning to the plight of those who don't fit in with the "cool" crowd. This drawing takes a different approach to the traditional drawing of Victor Frankenstein's nameless monster. In the original novel by Mary Shelley, the monster was tall, agile, and very strong, but also horribly deformed. Although Shelley's description of the creature is somewhat vague, he is described as looking like a corpse—we've stayed true to this vision. In this scene, a gang of villagers is chasing him.

Step One Start with a dynamic pose for the creature—shown here leaping over a ravine—by drawing simple shapes and a ball-jointed frame for the body.

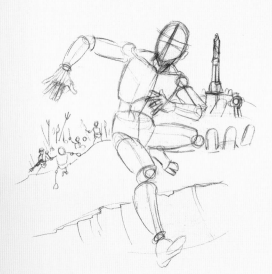

Step Two Start blocking in the body masses and filling in the extremities. Sketch in the lower-leg muscles and facial guidelines. Roughly sketch in the background elements and erase any unwanted sketch marks.

Step Three Keep in mind the distortions of this creature's face while sketching—his mismatched eyes and ears are asymmetrical. Add the facial features, and continue building up the muscle detail; then add hair and indicate the toes.

Step Four Begin drawing this creature's ill-fitting clothing, which reflects the early 1800s—the time period in which the novel was set. Continue to refine the face and body, and fill in the details of the angry mob in the background.

Step Five With an HB pencil, begin to darken the outline of the creature and refine the details. The main light source is coming from the upper left side of the frame; keep this in mind when you start to shade. Don't forget details such as bulging veins and the stitch lines on the hands, arms, and forehead. Draw the wrinkles and folds of the jacket using the techniques described in "Creating Texture" on page 95.

Step Six Continue to build up the details, including the rope belt around his waist. Refine the background, making sure that the directions of light and shadow are consistent. Add detail to the grave markers and leafless trees. Add shading to the crowd to suggest the impression of more detail. Draw smoke billowing up from the torches, as well as cracks in the ravine.

Step Seven Darken the outlines, and use a 2B pencil to refine spatial or anatomical details; then darken the deepest shadows.

Step Eight This palette consists of gray, blue, blue-gray, green, yellow, and earth tones. Art markers work especially well for this project and can be applied in layers or in small circular strokes. After the base color is down, you can add additional colors or introduce shading with colored pencils.

Werewolf

He crouches beneath a full moon, caught in the midst of transforming from man to beast. Living under a curse, the werewolf has no control over his animal nature once he has changed. You may note that he bears striking similarities to some of your fellow students during finals—and maybe even your parents when they get mad.

Step One Use a 2H pencil to block out the basic shape, positioning the legs so the creature appears to be midstride with the left leg slightly lifted. Use a ball-jointed wire frame to rough out the body.

Step Two Fill in the limbs and work in the prominent muscle groups, including the chest, shoulder, and abdomen. Begin adding details to the face and claws.

Step Three Continue to develop the details of the muscles, snout, ears, and eyes. Add loose sketch lines above the snout to give the appearance of a snarl. Rough in a pair of torn shorts and shreds of a ripped shirt. Sketch pine trees and a full moon in the background.

Step Four Use dark hatching to create the fur, keeping in mind the direction of the moonlight. Notice how a clear edge of reflected light has formed on the werewolf's arm by way of a narrow, lighter contour around the outer upper portion. You can create this effect by lifting out highlights in select places with a kneaded eraser.

Step Five Continue building up the inner form of the werewolf's chest and torso by adding more fur; then lift out highlights to create an illusion of light and shadow. Notice the effect of the moonlight on the top of the creature's head. Refine the details of his legs and shorts, adding shading and deeper tones on the right side of the upper and lower body. When drawing the outer contours, think about the basic nature of the shape you're drawing. For example, the werewolf's legs are essentially cylinders.

Step Six Continue to lift out highlights that correspond to the light source, including the faint backlighting on the lower legs. Smudge your pencil marks to soften the lines on the creature's torn jeans.

Step Seven Darken the pine trees and add a face to the moon. Lay down an even tone of pencil with fine strokes over the background. Then smudge slightly for a softer, more atmospheric look.

Step Eight This nighttime scene will give you the opportunity to explore how light plays on various forms. The scene is defined by dark- and medium-blue shadows and light-blue highlights. Notice how the light-blue side-lighting accentuates the beast's massive volume. A pale moon and the werewolf's blazing orange eyes help soften the dominant palette. For added dimension, feel free to add highlights using light dabs of white acrylic paint.

Goblin

Emerging from the cave he calls home, this towering goblin is ready to prowl the nearby woods for a mid-morning snack. He normally prefers full-grown humans—they have more meat on their bones, after all. But he's been known to chase after the local school bus when it's full—just one more reason to have your mom drive you. Taller than the nearby trees, this gruesome goblin should serve as a reminder not to stray off the marked path the next time you're in the woods.

Step One Sketch the figure using a ball-jointed wire frame. To keep the body in proportion, sketch the spine in the proper position—even though it will ultimately be covered in your final drawing. The goblin is a brutish creature, so draw his neck thrusting out, instead of aligned with his spine. Finally, rough in the tree form he is grasping.

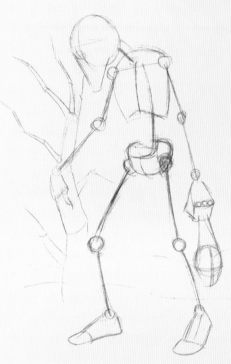

Step Two Now use simple lines and tapered cylinders to begin defining the arms and legs. Start developing the shape of the face and tree.

Step Three Using more contoured lines, begin filling in the thicker muscles. Draw in the outline of his clothes, and erase old sketch lines.

Step Four Sketch in jagged teeth, menacing eyes, and a few strands of hair. Don't forget his weapon, which is a large leg bone thrust into his belt. He also keeps a sack full of "trophies" tied to the other side. A necklace of finger bones adorns his upper body, while his latest prize—an unlucky fellow indeed—dangles from his left hand. When you compare the proportions of the goblin to his victim, you'll note that he is a bit on the gigantic side—somewhere around nine feet tall!

Step Five Now layer in the finer details of the creature's face, armbands, leggings, and sandals. Add a little more hair to his forehead and continue to refine the facial details. Notice how the muscles in his right thigh bulge slightly as they receive the weight of his body.

Step Six Begin fine tuning all of the details, including darkening the face, eyebrows, hair, and moustache; shading the neck, arm, and leg tendons and muscles; and refining the little details, such as the necklace made of human teeth and bones. The garment's folds have been indicated with shading and highlights. Add hair on the thighs and fur poking out from the leggings. Then add shadows where appropriate, such as beneath the hemline of his tunic.

Step Seven Finalize the remaining details of the figure and fill in the background. Details like trees and fog add to the overall dreadfulness of the goblin's lair, as do scraps of debris outside the mouth of his cave. Use your kneaded eraser to remove old sketch lines and then trace over the goblin one last time using a dark 2B pencil. Enhance the shadows, soften the transitions from light to dark, and darken the holding line around the creature to make him stand out from the background.

Step Eight The color scheme for the goblin employs subdued earth tones, except for the scarlet and orange in the background, which imply danger. The eye is drawn toward the goblin's lair, colored in mysterious dark blues. A mist partially obscures trophies from past meals, and the earthy colors of the ground suggest a somber, decaying place.

Bogeyman

You wouldn't want to see this guy lurking outside your bedroom window in the middle of the night. But that's exactly what a bogeyman might do—just for fun. On the other hand, he might hide under your bed and tickle your toes when you're trying to sleep. One thing's for sure, though: This scary guy is up to no good. Our bogeyman stands hunched over. He has long, claw-like hands and sharp teeth. This scrawny, spindly creature also delights in making your heart beat faster. He even likes it when you run away...screaming, of course.

Step One Use a light pencil to rough in a ball-jointed figure in a hunched-over stance. Note that the shape of the head is thin and angular. Use long pencil strokes to indicate his claw-like hands.

Step Two Begin to fill in the body volumes, and be sure to indicate the evil grin on his face. This monster takes a lot of pleasure in being creepy. Begin sketching in his long bony fingers—which he uses to snatch up disobedient children!

Step Three Now start roughing in the bogeyman's clothing to include a cape, a fedora, and an ill-fitting suit. Lightly sketch in the facial details, which should be skull-like in appearance, including piercing eyes, well-defined cheekbones, a pointy nose, and sharp teeth. His hair should be long and unruly.

Step Four Now clean up unnecessary sketch lines and begin to darken your outlines. Notice how the positions of his bent arms and legs define the shape of his jacket sleeves and pants. Darken the lines around the teeth, and draw the eyes with an evil look. To achieve this effect, slightly blur the irises and add a bit of tone to the whites. Next, add some drool dripping grotesquely from his jaw. Finally, sketch an outline of the ground shadow beneath him.

Step Five Begin lightly shading the areas on the bogeyman that appear to recede into the picture, such as the shadows under his cape. The hard-edged shadows on the figure further enhance the volume in the drawing.

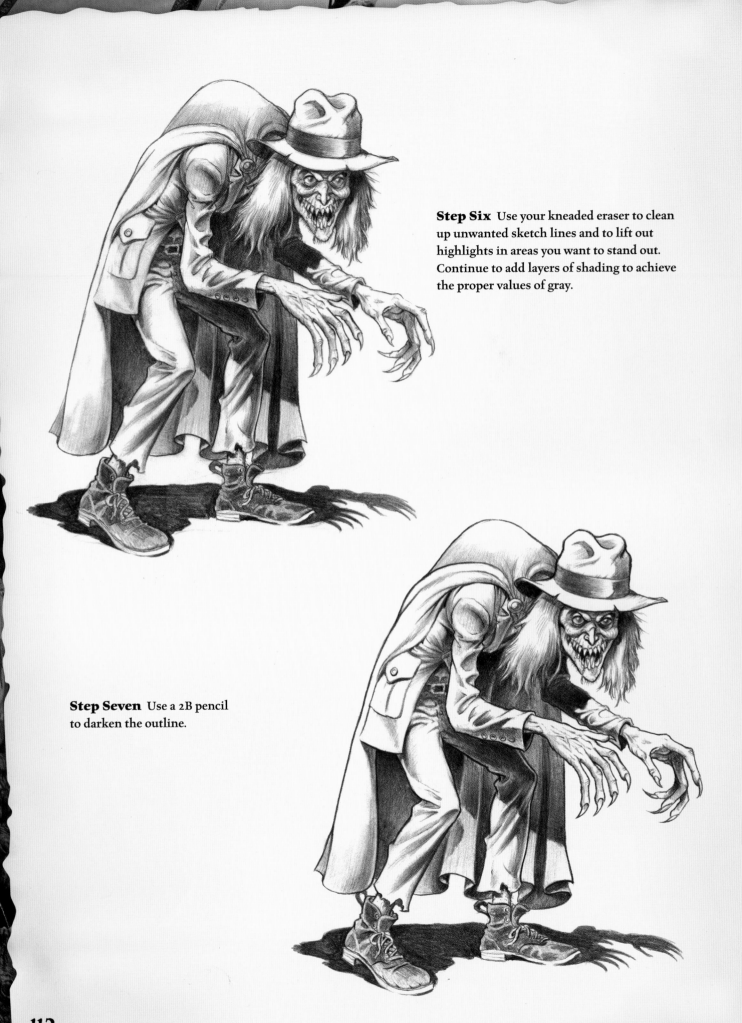

Step Six Use your kneaded eraser to clean up unwanted sketch lines and to lift out highlights in areas you want to stand out. Continue to add layers of shading to achieve the proper values of gray.

Step Seven Use a 2B pencil to darken the outline.

Step Eight Use a washed-out brown for the bogeyman's suit and shoes, and a warm gray for the beat-up fedora. Give the creature a deathly pallor by coloring his skin gray-green. The only colorful element should be the red cloak, an item that suggests he is deadly and dangerous. Color the background in dark blue punctuated by light-blue highlights to give a night-time feel to the scene. Add mysterious fog and faint rectangles to suggest an urban landscape.

Grim Reaper

This is one guy you never want to run into when you're out skateboarding. With a skeletal body, tattered clothes, and a gruesome grin, the Grim Reaper appears to love his job. By merely swinging his scythe, he brings death to all he passes. The Grim Reaper is sometimes depicted as a faceless wraith, wearing a flowing, hooded robe. In this drawing, however, we're bravely keeping his face—a creepy skull—openly visible.

Step One Rough in the basic body shape, which is somewhat cylindrical. He'll be swinging a scythe, so make sure you indicate this.

Step Two Now draw a basic skeleton form, paying attention to the relationship between the rib cage, pelvis, and spine. Start filling in the contours around the wire frame, and add guidelines to the face.

Step Three Begin sketching the details of the skull, making sure that the jaw line, mouth, eyes, and nose curve with the shape of the head. Continue to fill in the rib cage, maintaining its unique shape and volume (notice the dynamic arch in the spine). Finally, rough in the bony fingers gripping the long handle of the scythe.

Step Four Lightly sketch the Reaper's robe, which is loosely draped around his bony figure. Add long, scraggly hair and the rough shape of a belt made from a hangman's noose. Notice how the lower half of the Reaper's body seems to become integrated with the robe. Erase underlying sketch lines.

Step Five Begin darkening your line work and shading the rib cage, spine, and pelvis. Draw a chain intertwining with the noose belt, and begin shading parts of the face and hair.

115

Step Six Refine the scythe and the bony leg peeking out from under the torn robe. Shade in the edges of the robe, noting how the drawing begins to flatten out and appear more graphic. Complete the scythe, adding chips to the blade.

Step Seven Now shade the drawing liberally, noting how the interior of the robe is rendered in slightly lighter tones. This provides an atmospheric clue to the volume of space that fills the robe. Go over the entire drawing one final time using a 2B pencil. Darken key shadows and lines to enhance the figure overall. Use your kneaded eraser to remove old sketch lines, and lift out select highlights to indicate the direction of the light source.

Fine Lines

Pencil is an exciting medium for its versatility. Notice how small, swift strokes work together to create the texture of the Reaper's skull. A few horizontal strokes on the forehead add to the "expression," while a series of vertical strokes combined with shading just above the upper teeth indicate the shape and structure of the mouth.

TIP ❧ The tatters of the robe look a bit flame-like. Soften the ends so they look like wisps of smoke.

Step Eight This color palette consists of deep blue-green for the robe, light brown for the skeletal body, and light yellow for the noose. Apply dark brown to the handle of the scythe, and color the blades and his chain in blue-gray, using a bit of white to add highlights.

Swamp Creature

Whether the result of a science experiment gone wrong or the product of toxic dumping in the wetlands, this swamp creature has grown to monstrous proportions. Apparently, he's also grown tired of dining on tadpoles and catfish, for he's lumbered out of the water and is now heading toward the nearby summer camp. Here's hoping that you decided to stay home this year! This nocturnal creature is shown midstride as he emerges from the dark, muddy waters of the swamp.

Step One Draw simple shapes and a ball-jointed stick figure to establish the form. Position the center of the neck directly over the monster's supporting foot.

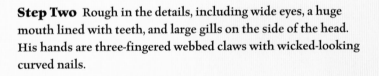

Step Two Rough in the details, including wide eyes, a huge mouth lined with teeth, and large gills on the side of the head. His hands are three-fingered webbed claws with wicked-looking curved nails.

Step Three Introduce faint lines to indicate the plates on his stomach and the shape of his webbed feet. Use your kneaded eraser to remove old sketch lines. This creature is amphibious and uses his gills to breathe underwater. On land, however, he breathes through his mouth through the aid of massive blood vessels that radiate from the center of his chest. Be sure to sketch in some faint lines to indicate these, as well.

Step Four Start sketching fish-like scales all over his body and further define the detail of his stomach plates. Refine the shape of his webbed feet so they look more grounded in the scene. Notice how the claws of the left foot spread out to help support his massive bulk, whereas the right foot appears slightly compressed. Sketch the swamp, a crescent moon, and a pair of fluttering bats in the background.

Step Five Begin tightening the line work with a darker HB pencil. Add shadows inside his mouth to emphasize his sharp teeth. Establish a light source by shading in select areas, such as his stomach and underneath his chin. Add a few spiny protrusions on the shoulders and chin. Then add shading around the veins, and begin filling in the scales.

Step Six Continue to develop the details of the creature's armor-plated stomach, as well as the veins on the front and sides of his body. Finish outlining the legs and feet, and continue filling in the scales.

Foreshortening

Foreshortening helps give an illusion of depth and perspective by making objects or elements in the foreground appear larger than objects and elements in the background. To ensure that the creature's scales appear to be a realistic part of his body—rather than float on the surface—be sure to draw them in different shapes and sizes, according to their placement. In other words, scales toward the front should be larger than scales toward the back.

Step Eight Add the final layers of shading to indicate the internal planes of the body. Notice how the upper-front parts of the legs are shaded lightly, while the lower-recessed parts are shaded in darker tones. Using the broad side of your pencil, loosely fill in the background details. Use a blending stump or your finger to soften the strokes for an atmospheric effect. Add slight ripples in the water, and darken the deepest areas of shadow. Trace over the outlines and darker shadow areas one last time with a 2B pencil.

Step Nine A natural color palette works best for this creature, who has emerged from the swamp right at sunset. The horizon is colored in orange and highlighted with a bit of yellow, whereas the color of the fog is blue and purple. Use various shades of green for the monster's body, punctuated by bits of orange in key places.

Loch Ness Monster

With a long neck and sinuous tail, the Loch Ness monster—which allegedly lives in a large, fresh-water lake in Scotland—bears a strange resemblance to the prehistoric Plesiosaurus: a dinosaur that lived during the Jurassic and Cretaceous periods. But everybody knows that dinosaurs are extinct, right? Our monster has the barrel-like body of a plesiosaurus, the head of a kelpie—or water horse—of Celtic legend, and the long undulating tail usually reported in most Loch Ness sightings.

Step One First rough out a circle for the head; a long, curvy cylindrical shape for the neck; and soft, rounded shapes for the body and tail. Finally, sketch in stubby, cylindrical legs; a rectangular snout; and fin-like ears.

Step Two Draw a thick brow ridge over small, beady eyes. Add nostrils and lips to the snout. Sketch thick, segmented scales across the stomach and sharp fins along the tail. Your creature will be emerging from the lake, so draw in a bit of splashing water around the legs.

Step Three Begin adding scales to the head and snout. Then add a scaly mane to the back of the neck and under the chin. Draw in curved teeth. This creature sports a diamond-shaped scale pattern, so start by lightly sketching crisscross guidelines around the body, following its shape and contours. Add more detail to the claws and draw an additional fin along the back. In the background, sketch in a ruined Scottish castle and the ripples of water beneath the creature's massive frame.

Step Four Using an HB pencil, begin darkening the final line work. Note the thick-scaled plates on the monster's snout and brow ridge. As you draw the contour lines of the body, give the lines some small waves to suggest the scales that you'll be adding in the next few steps. Work on the details of the splashing water and waves.

Step Five Draw a variety of uneven waves and ripples to capture the disruption in the water. Start filling in the diamond-shaped scale pattern. Note that the lower portion of each scale is shaded to create an illusion of solidity. You'll be creating this pattern all over the creature. By using a flattened point on your pencil, you can easily fill in the scale shading.

Step Six Continue to layer in the scale pattern. Scales that are in complete shadow should be shaded completely. This will be a nighttime scene, so the shadows should be very dark. Draw a full moon in the sky, which will also provide a light source. Note how the amount of shadow on each scale changes along with the curvature of the creature's body. Pay close attention to how the light falls on each section. The lower portion of the body is in deep shadow. The amount of shading decreases as more light falls upon that specific area.

Step Seven Complete the shading of the scale pattern. Lift out small highlights and use a bit of lighter shading to fully capture the volumes of the creature's large form. Note how the deepest shadows are in areas where light is unlikely to reach, such as the underside of her tail. The combination of the shading and the scale pattern works together to create an illusion of depth.

Step Eight Use a 2B pencil to darken the line work and tighten the shadows. Finally, using the HB pencil, lightly shade the Highlands in the background. Work a darker tone into the castle for atmospheric perspective. Use your kneaded eraser to create the fog by lifting out highlights.

Step Nine The Loch Ness monster rises in the dead of night, so the color palette should be dark and moody. Note how the moon helps add a tiny bit of light to the overall dark scene, as does a swath of green at the horizon and the light-blue highlights that help to define the monster's form. The stars in the sky also help to give the illusion of a vast outdoor space.